WITHDRAWN
AND
DONATED
FOR SALE

African Industries

WARREN J. HALLIBURTON

EDITED BY
SUSAN M. GROSSMAN

CRESTWOOD HOUSE
NEW YORK

MAXWELL MACMILLAN CANADA
TORONTO

MAXWELL MACMILLAN INTERNATIONAL
NEW YORK OXFORD SINGAPORE SYDNEY

ACKNOWLEDGMENTS

All photos courtesy of Magnum Photos.

Special thanks to Laura Straus for her assistance in putting this project together.

PHOTO CREDITS: COVER: *Eric Lessing; Marc Riboud* 4, 40, 47; *S. Salgado* 6, 18, 22, 26, 42; *Ian Berry* 9; *George Rodger* 10, 13, 14; *Stuart Franklin* 16; *Peter Marlow* 20; *Susan Meiselas* 25; *Eli Reed* 28; *Abbas* 30; *Rene Burri* 33; *Jean Gaumy* 36; *Alex Webb* 39

Cover design, text design and production: William E. Frost Associates Ltd.

Library of Congress Cataloging-in-Publication Data

Halliburton, Warren J.
    African industries / by Warren J. Halliburton; edited by Susan M. Grosssman. — 1st ed.
    p. cm. — (Africa today)
    Summary: An examination of the agricultural and industrial products of the African countries.
    ISBN 0-89686-672-6
    1. Africa—Economic conditions—1960- 2. Africa—Industries.
  3. Agriculture—Economic aspects—Africa. 4. Farm produce—Africa.
  I. Grossman, Susan M. II. Title. III. Series: Halliburton, Warren J.
Africa today
HC800.H34 1993
338.096—dc20   92-27325

Copyright © 1993 by CRESTWOOD HOUSE, MACMILLAN PUBLISHING COMPANY

All rights reserved. No part of this book may be reproduced or transmitted in any form or by any means, electronic or mechanical, including photocopying, recording, or by any information storage and retrieval system, without permission in writing from the Publisher.

CRESTWOOD HOUSE
MACMILLAN PUBLISHING COMPANY
866 Third Avenue
New York, NY 10022

MAXWELL MACMILLAN CANADA, INC.
1200 Eglinton Avenue East
Suite 200
Don Mills, Ontario M3C 3N1

Macmillan Publishing Company is part of the Maxwell Communication Group of Companies.
First edition
Printed in the United States of America

1   2   3   4   5   6   7   8   9   10

Contents

NOTE: The images in this book are meant to convey visually the spirit of the African industries, and are therefore not captioned. For full descriptions of the photos *see page 47*.

Introduction   7
    A Picture of Diversity
    The Forces of Change

1 African Agriculture: A Mixed Harvest   11
    The Cost of Colonization
    A Challenging Land
    Harvest of Tradition
    A Failure in Farming
    Strategies for Success
    Toward a Solution

2 Major Agricultural Commodities of Africa   21

3 African Industry: Wealth From the Earth   31

      An Abundance of Riches
      The Legacy of Colonization
      Problems of Supply and Demand
      Strategies for Improvement
      Foreign Investment

4 Major Industrial Commodities of Africa   37

Unexploited Wealth   43

Glossary   45

Index   48

Introduction

A Picture of Diversity

Consider these snapshots from Africa: in the first, Canadian combine harvesters roll across a wheat field in Tanzania; in another, three young men work on an oil rig in Angola. In the last, a 12-year-old refugee of war, bones showing and stomach swollen, lies dying in drought-stricken Ethiopia.

Each of these very different photographs would tell the truth about life in Africa. On one hand, Africa is a giant of a continent, packed with riches. It is a major provider of many of the earth's **minerals**, as well as several kinds of food products. Yet it is also a nation whose population is increasing more quickly than its ability to produce food. While it should be making money by **exporting** goods, Africa is forced to **import** food from other countries, piling up huge debts it has no way of paying. And while the majority of Africans make a living from farming, the government is pouring 80 percent of the national income into failing industries. Africa is a continent recently free from **colonization** facing competition from **industrialized** nations that its former rulers did not prepare it to keep up with.

The Forces of Change

Africans had been successfully supporting themselves as farmers, herders and craftspeople for thousands of years before encountering outside cultures. While Europe was still in its Dark Ages, great cities were rising in the western Sudan, and trade routes were winding through the African continent and along its coasts. Contact with foreign traders gave Africans new ideas to absorb. In turn, they were able to affect the people they met.

But years of living apart from other peoples did not prepare Africans for adapting to new conditions. Their way of life remained unchanged for thousands of years, while the world around them began to develop more and more technology. When people from other lands began to come to Africa in the 1400s seeking new territory, the Africans could not compete with their advanced technology. Then, when the slave trade began, many Africans were taken away from their homes, drastically reducing the number of people available to farm the land and develop new ways of living.

Colonization took even more Africans away from the traditional way of life. By 1920 all the African nations except Ethiopia, Liberia and the Union of South Africa had been claimed by European powers. The new rulers disrupted traditional African social and economic patterns without teaching the Africans new ways of living and competing with the industrialized world they had forced them to become a part of. While it is true that many of the colonizing nations introduced improved technology to the countries they took control of, they did not teach the people how to use it. When the African countries later gained independence, they found themselves unable to use the machinery their captors had left behind.

The countries of Africa must now live with the changes imposed on them by colonization. They have to learn how to switch from the traditional agricultural way of life to an industrial **economy**. In order to

command the future, Africans must be able to take the valuable resources of their continent and make them work in today's competitive world trade market.

African Agriculture: A Mixed Harvest

The Cost of Colonization

Africa is a continent in an agricultural crisis. Its population is increasing while its ability to feed itself is decreasing. There are many reasons for this, the main one being the lasting effects of colonization. Most African nations have become free from colonial rule only in the last 40 years. When the ruling powers left, African people who were used to living in individual villages and tribes suddenly had to look at themselves as part of a country. They had difficulty in forming stable governments, because the members of different **ethnic** groups disagreed on what needed to be done and who should be in charge.

In addition, most of the African countries are reluctant to develop the tools necessary to support industries and economies that they had no hand in creating. The challenge faced by Africa is to develop over a few years the technology that other parts of the world have had many decades to develop.

A Challenging Land

The ability of African land to support farming varies as widely as the nature of the land itself. The largest desert in the world, the Sahara, covers much of northern Africa, while seven percent of the continent's most fertile land is hidden under lush forests, unavailable for use. Between these two extremes, the quality of land varies from place to place.

Ironically, the need for more space for growing food or grazing animals can destroy the land's ability to support life. Farming without the use of **fertilizer** drains the soil of nutrients. Grazing animals can strip an area bare, causing **desertification**.

In all, only 19 percent of Africa's land is presently capable of supporting crops. Of this land, only 4.4 percent is **irrigated** below the Sahara Desert. And of the land that is irrigated for farming, 75 percent is found in only four countries. This means that the majority of African countries either do not have land capable of growing food or, if they do have it, they do not have the ability to keep it watered.

Harvest of Tradition

In defiance of these grim facts, most Africans continue to live as farmers. Many are **subsistence farmers**, using what they grow for themselves. Traditionally, farming is a family project. Men prepare the land for planting, and women do the planting and tend to the crops. Men usually grow crops that can be sold for profit, while women produce food to be eaten by the family or traded at local markets.

Today African farming continues to resemble the farming methods used for centuries. The most common farming tools are still a hoe and a knife. Most farmers cannot afford machinery, fertilizer or insecticides. Despite these outdated conditions, Africa leads the world in the production of cocoa, **cassava**, cashews, cloves, palm oil, pyrethrum (a natural insecticide), vanilla beans and yams. It is also a major source of bananas,

coffee, cotton, peanuts, rubber, sugar and tea. Africa raises two-thirds of the world's camels, one-third of its goats and one-seventh of its sheep and cattle.

A Failure In Farming

As the population of Africa increases, more and more land is being devoted to agriculture. Unfortunately, this is often at the expense of wildlife, natural habitats and human residents. This has increased the amount of crops African countries produce, sometimes even creating a **surplus** of some goods. Still, this is not enough to keep up with the demands of a growing population. Between the mid-1970s and the mid-1980s, foreign food aid to Africa tripled, and imports of wheat, corn and rice doubled.

As it gets harder and harder to live by farming, many Africans are moving to the cities. These people have very low incomes and must spend what money they do have on buying the food they were unable to grow in their villages. Many African governments are encouraging the growth of cities, hoping that it will increase Africa's industries. This has created a situation in which 80 to 90 percent of a country's national budget is being spent on industries that employ only about 10 to 30 percent of the population. When an industry begins to fail, even more money is spent to save it, taking money away from agriculture.

The farmers that do remain have been forced to change from **subsistence farming** to producing **cash crops** that can be sold for a profit. However, because of bad weather conditions, civil wars, poor government management policies, and changes in the world demand for cash crops, most farmers cannot count on making a steady income.

Strategies For Success

African governments have attempted to solve the problem of inadequate food production in two ways: by combining small farms (called **smallholdings**) into larger **collective farms**, and by teaching farmers more modern techniques for growing crops.

In the years after colonization ended, many African countries promoted the organization of collective farms. This meant that many small farms that struggled to survive would be joined into one large farm, with everyone pitching in to run things.

In theory, working as a collective has many advantages. Knowledge and equipment can be shared, and things like machinery, seed, fertilizer and insecticides can be bought more easily when money is shared.

But the success of a collective farm also depends on people working together to make things run smoothly, and this has not happened. Most of the cooperative farms set up by African governments have failed. They suffer from poor management and lack of basic materials and technical support. Also, many workers prefer to spend time tending their own plots rather than working on the larger plots that support the group. Ethiopia is the only African country where collective farming is widely practiced.

Recently, many governments have decided to return to a system of private land ownership, where individuals own and work their own farms. They are supporting small farmers by offering financial assistance, making fertilizer available, teaching new farming methods and giving more land to farmers who do well.

These new methods are promising, but they have a long way to go. Many farms still fail due to lack of proper planning, equipment and technical assistance. And there is some resistance to the new crops that are being developed. For example, yellow corn is much easier to grow and produces more food than other types of corn. But attempts to introduce yellow corn in Africa failed because most Africans prefer to eat white corn.

Even if a crop is successful, there are other problems. Most African countries have very poor roads and few railways. This makes it hard for farmers to transport their crops to markets or to ports that ship products to other countries. And sometimes the success of a crop can be a disadvantage. If many farmers are growing the same kind of crop, then the market becomes flooded, and there is no demand for the food.

Toward A Solution

If African farms are to produce more food, then there have to be changes in the way the farms are run. More technical training and education are needed to show farmers how to run their farms effectively. Although Africa receives money from many different countries, this short-term aid does little to help farmers in the long run. Solving the puzzle of how to feed Africa's growing population would be a challenge for any nation. It is especially challenging for a continent undergoing change as rapidly as Africa is.

Major Agricultural Commodities of Africa

Cassava (manioc, tapioca): Native to South and Central America and introduced to Africa in the 1500s, cassava is the starchy root of a woody shrub. This food provides the dietary needs for more than 200 million people in Africa. African farms grow more than 50 percent of the world's cassava crop, yet almost none of the crop is sold outside the continent. Most is eaten by subsistence farmers. The leaves of the cassava plant are also nutritious, and are eaten as vegetables in some countries. Cassava will grow where other plants won't, and it needs no fertilizer or insecticides. It can also be left in the ground for up to two years, making it a valuable crop in times of famine. Industrial uses for cassava are also being developed. A mixture of cassava alcohol and gasoline can be used as motor fuel.

Cocoa: Also imported from Central and South America, cocoa trees are grown mainly in western Africa. Cocoa is used primarily in the manufacture of chocolate. After sugar and coffee, cocoa is Africa's most important agricultural product.

Coconut: Introduced to western Africa from the Asian Pacific, coconut palm trees are grown both as cash crops and subsistence crops, mostly in small garden plots. All parts of this plant are used. The fibers of the shell are combed out to produce **coir**, a stiff, ropelike fiber. The milk inside the nut is drunk. The "meat" inside the coconut can be eaten. It can also be dried and used as the source of **copra**, an oil used in soap, detergent, cosmetics, edible oils and margarine. Copra is also used in animal feed. Coconut oil is used in foods and is being studied as a possible source of diesel fuel. The coconut shell can also be crushed and used as industrial filler, and may be processed into a coal that could possibly be used as a low-polluting fuel.

Coffee: Following oil, coffee is the most profitable **commodity** on the world trade market. In Africa—which provides about 20 percent of the world's coffee—it is grown on small farms and is almost exclusively an export crop. Very few Africans drink coffee. Yet while coffee is a successful cash crop, many of Africa's coffee bushes are growing old and must be replaced if the nation is to keep its place in the world market.

Cotton: Cotton is a major source of income and employment in Africa. It can be sold both in its raw form and as yarn, fabric and clothing. The short hairs left on the seeds after the cotton is removed are used in paper, chemicals and explosives.

Cottonseed: This crop is used primarily in cattle feed, fertilizer and fuel. It can also be used in cooking oil, soap and margarine. Cottonseed products can also be eaten as a source of protein. However, processing cottonseed produces **gossypol**, a poisonous substance. While gossypol can be used in paints, industrial oils and rubber, efforts are under way to develop gossypol-free cotton.

Fishing: Commercial fishing is big business in Africa. Anchovies, mackerel, sardines, tuna and other fish are caught along the miles of seacoast. Much of the ocean fish is processed for fish oil and fish meal, and sold on the world market. Freshwater fish are usually sold and eaten locally.

Forestry: The African lumber industry, led by production in Nigeria, ranks eighth in the world. Exported woods include hardwoods such as walnut and mahogany and softwoods such as eucalyptus. Wood is also used locally for building and fuel. Unfortunately, lumber production in Africa is destroying the continent's forests, which are disappearing at the rate of 2 to 6 percent each year. As land is cleared by forestry, the soil erodes away. Every year in Africa an area of land twice the size of New Jersey becomes unproductive desert due to forest destruction.

Groundnut (peanut, monkey nut, earth nut): This crop is actually an herb from South America. It is the most important of Africa's oil-producing plants and is grown for both local use and export. The oil is edible and can also be used in soap and animal feed. Groundnut shells can also be converted into an inexpensive fertilizer.

Maize (Indian corn, mealie): The third most important world crop behind wheat and rice, maize is important as a food product in Africa. In the 1980s Africa supplied 7.5 percent of the world's maize. Now it is used mainly as a subsistence crop, and little is sold outside the continent.

Oil Palm: Palm oil is made from the pulp of this tree, grown primarily in western Africa, and palm kernel oil is made from the seed. Palm

oil has many uses, in margarine, as shortening, in ice cream, chocolate, soaps and detergents. Palm kernel oil is used in soaps and fats. In Africa palm trees grow wild, and most of the oil is used locally. As with coffee, many of Africa's palm trees are aging and must be replaced. Also, many countries do not have the technical ability to refine enough palm oil to sell it successfully on the world market.

Pyrethrum: The flowers of this herb, imported in 1929 from Yugoslavia, contain chemicals known as **pyrethrins,** which are poisonous to insects and used in insecticides. The world's leading producer of the herb, Kenya, supplies 65 to 75 percent of the world's market but is now being threatened by synthetic insecticides, which are cheaper. Pyrethrum is grown mostly in small plots on collective farms.

Sisal: The leaf of this plant, introduced in the late 1800s to what is now Tanzania, yields fibers used to make rope and twine products. Once the leading producer of sisal, Tanzania has been replaced by Brazil due to failed efforts at forming cooperative farms and lack of equipment. Kenya is now becoming an important producer of the product, but lacks the technology to process the raw sisal into a final product.

Sugar: Many plants produce sugar, but all manufactured sugar comes from sugarcane, introduced from Polynesia. Sugar has many uses besides as a sweetener. In view of rising petroleum prices and falling supplies, a promising use of sugarcane juice is in producing a motor fuel known as gasohol. Processing plants are being developed in Kenya, Malawi, South Africa, Zambia and Tanzania. What's left of the cane after it is crushed in processing can be burned as a fuel or used in paper and other **cellulose products** much as wood pulp is. South Africa, the principal African producer and exporter, has established a paper mill that uses sugarcane.

Sweet Potatoes and Yams: Nigeria produces 70 percent of the world's output of these starchy tubers.

Tea: Most tea is exported by India and Sri Lanka, but African tea accounts for about 20 percent of the world market. Kenya, one of the East's fastest-growing competitors, has been ranked fourth since 1975 in the export of black tea, most of it grown on small plantations.

Tobacco: In Africa this South American plant is grown mainly on large farms in Zimbabwe, Malawi and South Africa. In other parts of Africa it is a small farmer's crop, grown alongside other cash and subsistence crops.

African Industry: Wealth From the Earth

An Abundance of Riches

Excluding South Africa, Africa is the least industrialized region of the world. Most of its agriculture is produced only for subsistence. The few products it does export must be sold in their raw state, since most African nations do not have the technology to process raw materials into finished goods.

Yet Africa possesses an amazing percentage of the world's minerals. The African earth holds 90 percent of the world's cobalt, 80 percent of its chromium, one-third of its aluminum, most of its diamonds and one-third of its uranium, just to name a few. South Africa alone is incredibly rich with minerals, including aluminum, chromium, coal, diamonds, uranium, gold, 80 percent of the world's manganese and 90 percent of its platinum.

But despite the abundance of natural resources, most of African industry is what is known as **light industry**. The manufacturing of food, beverages, tobacco, textiles, clothing and leather accounts for about 60 percent of industrial employment. These industries are based on what products are in demand in the countries that produce them. They also require very little technology and education.

Unfortunately, they do require a great amount of work. And they are often affected by problems such as interruptions in power or water supplies and, as with farming, difficulties in transporting goods to buyers.

The other 40 percent of Africa's industries are **heavy industries**—chemical, petroleum, coal, rubber and metal production. However, these industries have been declining steadily since the 1970s due to problems such as civil war, poor management and the inability to keep up with changing technology.

The Legacy of Colonization

The nations of Africa do not even come close to filling their **export potential**. As with agriculture, this is partly caused by the fact that most African nations were, until recently, run by foreign countries for their own gain. While these colonial powers exploited African workers to run plantations and do physical work, they seldom taught them how to use the technology they were helping to support. When colonization ended, the African workers were left with no knowledge of the industries their efforts had fueled.

As a result, there is a serious shortage of people with technical and managerial skills in Africa. This leads to mistakes such as putting a factory in a location to which raw materials cannot be transported, or building machinery without any possibility of obtaining the spare parts to fix it when it breaks.

Because of these problems, most African industries have to rely on non-Africans for technical and managerial assistance. This prevents Africans from entering the industrial market and learning the skills they need to run a business.

Small businesses are also scarce in Africa. This is partly the result of limited financial resources and partly because of unhelpful government policies. This creates problems because the large industries then have no one to sell their products to. Also, since most Africans still live by subsistence farming, they do not have money to buy the things created by industry.

Problems of Supply and Demand

There are also more basic problems. The fact is that the earth's minerals are being used up. The earth cannot produce new supplies as quickly as we consume them. And Africa's mines are not going to produce forever.

Another problem facing African industry is the increasing competitiveness from other countries. Other developing nations are able to produce the same products for less money, and therefore are more attractive to importers. These countries are also able to keep more of the profits from sales. This money can then be put back into developing better technology.

The world is also finding substitutes for some of the resources African countries count on for profits. The demand for petroleum, one of Africa's major industries, has declined, as has the demand for coal. Ghana, which has huge reserves of bauxite, the ore used to produce aluminum, is having trouble selling it. Existing aluminum can be recycled for only 5 percent of the energy it takes to turn raw bauxite into finished aluminum.

Strategies for Improvement

As with farming, the success of industry in Africa varies from country to country. This depends on differences in available natural resources and the success of management programs. Many countries have recently turned their attention to improving existing industries rather than creating new ones. And some countries are moving away from relying on foreign goods, trying to support themselves through local industry. Some African countries have even tried to pool their resources. But this has met with limited success, largely because of the different levels of industrialization in each country.

In an effort to increase the level of efficiency in industry, some African countries are starting to focus on small and medium-sized businesses as sources of employment. These smaller businesses can produce simple goods to be used by the people in the country. They also provide a training ground for people to develop management skills. Once the basic skills are learned, larger businesses can be started and maintained without as much dependence on outside help.

Foreign Investment

Industry in Africa has, until recently, existed without the help of **foreign investment**. In 1989, for instance, Singapore received almost twice as much foreign aid as all of Africa.

There are various reasons for this. Many African governments have not been friendly to foreign governments. This prevented other countries from supplying Africa with money to start and run businesses. Investors have also been uncomfortable about investing money in countries where the government is unstable, as is the case with many African countries.

In recent years, however, many African governments have begun to seek out foreign investors. With changes in laws and attitudes, perhaps more countries will begin to support African businesses.

Major Industrial Commodities of Africa

Aluminum: Aluminum, extracted from bauxite ore, is used as an abrasive and in glass and ceramics. Its by-products are used in plastics and as a fire retardant in carpet backing. One-third of the world's bauxite reserves are in Ghana. Cameroon refines the aluminum produced in Ghana.

Chromium: The main use of this element is in stainless steel. South Africa contains 70 percent of the world's known reserves, and Zimbabwe possesses another 10 percent.

Coal: Coal, the only mineral fuel found in South Africa, has overtaken diamonds as the country's chief export. It also fills 80 percent of that country's energy needs. South Africa is the only country in the world that has experience in distilling fuel oil from coal.

Cobalt: Zaire possesses 65 percent of the world's cobalt, a metallic element used in making high-grade steel, aircraft and industrial engines and magnets.

Copper: Used primarily as an electrical conductor, this metal is increasingly being replaced by aluminum due to the expense and complexity of its production. It is the main export of Zambia, which along with Zaire, accounts for 12 percent of the world's reserves. Soon these countries will have to find other industries. It is expected that the world's copper reserves will be depleted by 2010.

Diamonds: Zaire was the world leader in diamond production until 1983, when it was overtaken by Australia. But the country is still the largest producer in Africa. Diamonds are also Botswana's main export. Its mining company, the De Beers Botswana Mining Company, is owned jointly with South Africa. South Africa's diamond production has been declining, as has Tanzania's. Namibia's diamond mines are not expected to be profitable after 2000. And in other countries the diamond trade is being destroyed by smuggling.

Gold: This element was first discovered in Africa in 1884 near Johannesburg, South Africa, and formed the base for that country's present wealth. But South Africa's aging mines are decreasing in profitability. In 1989 for the first time South Africa made more income exporting other goods than it did from gold. South Africa also faces competition from other countries.

Iron Ore: The bulk of mined iron is converted to steel by removing the carbon found in the element. Stainless steel is produced by adding other metals. Iron ore is found throughout Africa. Gabon has one of the largest iron ore reserves in the world, and it has yet to be mined. The African country most dependent on iron as its source of export income is Mauritania, but its deposits are becoming exhausted. Before civil war disrupted their plans, Guinea and

Liberia planned to open a joint iron-mining venture. Other countries also have rich deposits of iron and are working to make them profitable. Tanzania is seeking funding for a coal and steel complex. Angola, where production has been halted by war, is expected to resume mining once an adequate transportation system between the mines and the coast is set up.

Manganese: South Africa is the world's leading exporter of this element used in steel manufacturing. South Africa and the former Soviet Union combined to account for over 80 percent of the world's reserves of this element. It is also the leading export of Gabon. Ghana, assisted by a loan from the World Bank, is Africa's other major exporter.

Petroleum: Petroleum reserves throughout Africa make up almost 10 percent of the world's oil. It is Nigeria's main source of income. Many other African countries are believed to have oil reserves, but they lack the technology to find and make use of them.

Phosphates: This element, used mainly in the manufacturing of fertilizer, detergents, animal feed, insecticides, matches and ceramics, is found mainly in Morocco, which possesses 50 percent of the world's reserves. But some European countries have banned the use of phosphates in agriculture because they pose an environmental threat. What effect this will have on African trade has yet to be seen.

Platinum: This metal is mainly used in manufacturing catalytic converters, which reduce air pollution from exhaust emissions. As environmental issues continue to become more and more important, the demand for platinum is expected to increase. South Africa dominates world production, filling 90 percent of the need for platinum.

Tin: Some of the world's main deposits of this metal are found in the equatorial zones of Africa.

Uranium: South Africa is one of the world's leaders in reserves of this element, used mostly as fuel for the production of nuclear power and nuclear weapons. Since 1989, however, Niger has surpassed South Africa in export. Uranium is also produced in Namibia and Gabon, and has been found in several other countries.

Unexploited Wealth

Africa is a continent whose unexploited riches include not only the minerals and fruits of the earth but the talents of its people. Africans must be educated in the use of modern technology so that they can sustain the industries developed by their former colonial rulers and also explore new opportunities. Failing industries must be examined to see if they can be revitalized. Countries that are dependent on only a few resources need to find other means of supporting themselves.

Subsistence farmers and small businesspeople need to be supported with both increased financial aid and increased education. It also seems that Africa does not suffer so much from a lack of food as it does from inadequate ways of distributing the food it produces across the continent.

However, making these issues priorities requires some stability on a country's part. Ever-changing political structures and constant threats of war make it difficult for African countries to establish stability, especially when it comes to economic matters. If Africa and her people are to become leaders in the world trade market, it will take a great deal of work on the part of the African people and support from the rest of the world.

Glossary

Cash crops   Crops grown and sold for a profit.
Cassava   A starchy root used as a source of protein.
Cellulose products   Products, like paper, made from wood fibers.
Coir   A stiff, ropelike fiber made from the hair of coconut shells.
Collective farms   Large farms created by combining several smaller farms into one.
Colonization   The act of a country taking control of a piece of land and claiming the land as its own.
Commodity   Any goods that can be sold for profit.
Copra   An oil made from coconut that is used in soaps and other products.
Desertification   The process by which fertile land is turned into desert due to overuse and erosion.
Economy   The financial state of a country, which is affected by how much money is coming into and going out of the country.

Ethnic groups Groups that are related based on common background and heritage.
Export The process of selling goods grown or made in a country to other countries for a profit.
Export potential The ability of a country to make money by selling goods or services to other countries.
Fertilizer Anything used to replace the nutrients in the earth that are used up by growing plants.
Foreign investment Getting other countries to put money into businesses or industry.
Gossypol A poisonous substance created from processing raw cotton.
Heavy industry Industries, such as chemical, petroleum, coal and metal production, that require the use of factories or large machinery.
Import The process of buying from another country goods or services that are not available locally.
Industrialized Having the technology and ability to produce goods efficiently for resale.
Insecticides Anything used to prevent bugs from destroying crops.
Irrigated To be supplied with enough water to allow crops to grow.
Light industry Industries, such as food, textile, or tobacco production, that do not require a lot of technology or use of heavy machinery.
Minerals Substances found in nature that are mined and used to create other products.
Pyrethrins Chemicals found in the flowers of the herb pyrethrum.
Smallholdings Small, privately owned farms.
Subsistence farmers Farmers who use the crops they grow only to feed their families, not to sell for profit.
Surplus Food or goods that are left over after the amount needed to survive has been used.

PHOTO IDENTIFICATION

(Cover) A copper processing plant\Rhodesia; (4) using animals to plow a field\Algeria; (6) a market scene in Yaounde\Cameroon; (9) threshing wheat with outdated equipment\Ethiopia; (10) harvesting wheat near the Sahara\Algeria; (13) an irrigation system\Algeria; (14) a camel draws water from a well\Algeria; (16) cabbages and peppers growing in a garden project\Burkina Faso; (18) a palm oil plantation\Cameroon; (20) cassava plants\Nigeria; (22) a cocoa plantation\Cameroon; (25) fishing\Mozambique; (26) a palm oil plantation\Cameroon; (28) a tea plantation\Malawi; (30) a gold miner\Ghana; (33) a rubber factory\Liberia; (36) diamonds\Sierra Leone; (39) a copper mine\Zaire; (40) a construction project\Algeria; (42) unloading shrimp boats\Cameroon; (47) a herd of sheep in the Sahara\Algeria

Index

agriculture   11–19, 31
aluminum   34, 37

bauxite   34, 37
Botswana   38

cassava   12, 21, 45
chromium   37
coal   37
cobalt   38
cocoa   12, 23
coconut   23
coffee   15, 23
coir   23, 45
collective farms   15, 17, 45
colonization   8, 11, 32, 45
copper   38
copra   23
cotton   15, 23
cottonseed   23

De Beers Botswana Mining Company   38
deforestation   24
desertification   12
diamonds   38

Ethiopia   8

fishing   24
foreign aid   15, 35
forestry   24

Gabon   38, 41
gasohol   27
Ghana   34, 37, 41
gold   38
gossypol   23, 24, 46
groundnut   24
Guinea   38

heavy industry   32, 46

industry   31–35
iron ore   38, 40

Kenya   27, 29

Liberia   8, 40
light industry   32, 46

maize   24
Malawi   27, 29
manganese   41
Mauritania   38
minerals   31, 34, 46
Morocco   41

Namibia   38, 41
Niger   41
Nigeria   24, 29, 41

palm oil   12, 24, 27
petroleum   41
phosphates   41
platinum   41
population   11, 15
pyrethrum   12, 27

Sahara Desert   12
sisal   27
small business   34, 35, 43
South Africa   8, 27, 29, 31, 37, 38, 41
stainless steel   38
subsistance crop   23, 24
subsistance farming   12, 15, 21, 43
sugar   13, 27
sweet potatoes   29

Tanzania   27, 38, 40
tea   15, 29
tin   41
tobacco   29
transportation   17

uranium   41

World Bank   41

yams   12, 29

Zaire   38
Zambia   27, 38
Zimbabwe   29, 37

48